I0450757

Chains of Light

Elizabeth Schechter

Published by Elizabeth Schechter, 2020.

Table of Contents

Chapter 1 | In the Thraya 1

Chapter 2 | Outside the Doors 14

Chapter 3 | The Heart of the Temple 24

Chapter 4 | The Man who Fights 36

Chapter 5 | On the Offensive 46

Chapter 6 | Freed 57

Chapter 7 | To Serve the Sorcerer 67

Chapter 1
In the Thraya

The late afternoon sun slanted through the high windows of the silent Thraya, setting motes of dust aglow like tiny stars as they floated through the air and settled on the silken and velvet cushions and draperies. The single occupant of the enormous room ignored the finery around him. He shook his dark hair back off his shoulders, focusing on the book settled on his folded legs. He read in silence, the quiet broken only by an occasional, faintly musical jingle. The source of the sound was the reader himself, as he shifted to turn pages, moving one hand forward and tucking the other behind his back with the ease of long practice. His movements made the jeweled chains that bound his wrists sparkle in the sunlight, casting blood-red shadows across the pages as he returned his palms to his thighs, fingertips just resting on the edges of the large tome.

From somewhere overhead, a deep gong sounded. The reader looked up, his expression one of mild surprise. He took hold of the volume in both hands as he unfolded his legs and stood, his long silken loincloth fluttering down around his knees as he moved. He set the book down and turned away from the couch in time to see the heavy doors swing open, revealing an armored woman and a man carrying a tray.

"Lyander, I'm sorry I'm so late," the man called as the guard pulled the door closed behind him. He moved toward a table, revealing a pronounced limp as he walked. He set the tray down on the table and started setting up the meal. Lyander watched him. He'd had other attendants before Delan, and while he knew he didn't know enough to compare, he did. He didn't have Trivir's simplicity, or Aniki's startling contrasts of pale hair and dark eyes. He certainly didn't have Jyase's startling dark beauty. Compared to them, Delan was a sparrow, or a wren – plain, solid, and brown in both hair and eyes. And, in Lyander's eyes, he was perfect. "I hope you're not too hungry?"

"Starved," Lyander answered, smiling and coming over to the table. "I was starting to think I'd mislaid my days again and it was a fast day." He glanced over his shoulder, toward the door that led out to his walled garden. "Delan, what is happening out there? I could hear shouting from the garden when I went out to feed the birds, but I couldn't hear anything clearly and I don't like to stay out there for very long."

"Ah, never you mind it, Holiness." Delan turned and leaned against the table. "It's nothing. Some upstart warlady, the Holy Mother says."

"A warlady marching against the Temple?" Lyander gasped. "Is she insane? Eldest Sister will take her apart!"

"So the Holy Mother says. So the Warrior grants. Eat now, while it's still hot. Then perhaps we'll see to other things..." Delan smiled, reaching out to brush his fingers over Lyander's cheek. "There's time before the sunset meditations."

Lyander shivered at the light in Delan's eyes, and sat down at the table, letting Delan uncover bowls and set them down. Then he tucked his left hand into the small of his back, pressed up against the metal loop on the belt locked around his waist that held fast the chain connecting his wrists. That allowed him enough movement in his right hand to eat, and he set to with enthusiasm, only to stop after a moment to look up at the young man watching him.

"Sit down, Delan. Share with me."

In the months since Delan had first come to the Temple and been appointed to serve in the Thraya, Lyander had made the offer at every meal. His previous attendant had always accepted; Delan, for some reason always refused. "I'm honored, Holiness, but the Holy Mother would have my hide if she knew."

"She wouldn't, Delan," Lyander said. He shook his head and started eating again. "She sends you to share my bed, why shouldn't you share my meals?"

"That's different," Delan said, turning away and limping across the room, the uneven sounds of his steps echoing from the high ceilings. "I don't understand how you can live like this."

"Like what?" Lyander asked. "In the Thraya? This is how sons of the Warrior Goddess have always lived. Didn't you know that?"

"No. So far as the people outside the temple know, there aren't any men in here. Shocked me silly the day I met you. I just — you're alone! And they keep you chained like a beast! Even outside the Temple, the men don't live like this. How can you stand it?" Delan turned back, his arms spread wide. "There's enough room here for... what? Two dozen men and boys? More? And yet—"

Lyander looked around, trying to remember when there had been someone else here besides him. When last there had been another male in the Thraya. After a moment, he shook his head and admitted defeat. "There used to be that many, but it was a long time ago. Or so I've been told. When the Warrior Goddess' Temple was first among all and the Warrior's bloodline was stronger. Then? Well, you know the history. I don't have to tell you about the holy wars. Now, I'm a Temple-born male, the last male of the Warrior's bloodline unless Eldest Sister decides to take a consort and somehow bears a son. I don't know if Brina will do either. She's near to being too old to carry a child safely. I've heard this year at the spring rites, I'll stand at my Mother's side—"

"And be nothing more than a stud set among the mares. I've heard that, too." Delan shook his head and repeated, "How can you stand it?"

"I could ask the same of you, Delan." Lyander laid down his spoon and rested his hand on the table. "I have my books. I study the ancient lore and the mysteries. I have the birds who live in my garden. I have the Temple sisters at meditations, and Eldest Sister and the Holy Mother." He looked up at Delan and smiled, adding, "And I have you. What else do I need?"

"What about your freedom?" Delan asked. "I have more freedom than you do, and I'm just a servant to the Temple. You're the Holy Mother's own son!"

Lyander blinked in surprise. "I was dedicated to the Temple the day I was born. I'm to be the Warrior's Consort. I'll sit at her right hand—" He stopped and wondered if he'd said too much, then shook his head. "That's been my destiny, always." He sighed and looked at the half-finished meal. "Delan, come and eat with me. They always send more than I can finish and Jyase always ate with me. I miss the company."

Delan hesitated for a moment, then came closer. "I'll sit—"

"Delan!"

"All right. I'll eat something." Delan sat down across from Lyander and picked up a piece of bread. "What else did he do? Jyase, you said his name was?"

"Yes. You haven't met him?"

Delan shook his head, spraying crumbs across the table. "No. They told me when I came looking for a place that your last attendant left the Temple before the first harvest started. Went to the army, from what gossip I heard."

Lyander went silent for a moment, stunned. Then he murmured, "They never told me. All I knew was he stopped coming. One of the Sisters brought my food, for a long while. Then you came. I didn't know he had left the temple. I thought he might have tired of me."

"Ah...shit," Delan whispered, his face suddenly pale. "Lyander, I'm sorry. I didn't know."

Lyander nodded, his eyes never leaving his hand. "Thank you. You should eat while the food is hot."

Lyander heard movement across the table, then felt pressure under his chin as Delan reached across and cupped Lyander's chin with his hand. Lyander looked up to see Delan, studying him with an unusual-for-him seriousness in his eyes. "I'm not leaving you," Delan said firmly. "I'm sorry he hurt you. You cared about him, I can see that. He obviously didn't deserve it. And you should eat, too."

"Oh." Lyander studied his bowl and pushed the bits of potato and carrots around. "Do you mean that?"

"That I'm not leaving?" Delan asked. "Yes, I mean that. I like it here. And I like you. I'm not going anywhere. Now eat and stop chasing it around."

Obediently, Lyander took another bite of stew, then laid his spoon down and took a piece of bread when Delan offered it to him. As he ate, he watched Delan, who was eating heartily.

"Tell me about yourself?" Lyander asked. "Before you came to the Temple, what were you?"

"Dirt-poor and starving," Delan answered immediately. "I don't imagine you know about the famines?"

"No!" Lyander answered in surprise. "Famines? Really? Is that why we have fast days so often? Tell me, is it very bad?"

"Yes." Delan nodded, staring past Lyander at something only he could see. "You plant your crops, they either don't come up at all or die before they're anywhere near harvest. I can't remember the last time it really rained during the growing seasons. Or at all, really. The winters come sooner, and they get harder every year. You set your animals to pasture, maybe half of them come back at sunset. Predators come on two legs and four, and there are babies dying, too weak even to cry. The Temples do what they can when they aren't fighting each other. But there are a lot of us in need and not enough help to go around. The Priestesses of the Light, they're more interested in their tithes than in helping the people, and there aren't many Temples of the Warrior anymore. I was lucky to find this one when I needed help." Delan shook his head. "Yes, it's bad and getting worse. There are warbands roaming wild, raiding the farms and villages for whatever they can find. Food. Money. Conscripts." He stopped and frowned.

"Delan?"

"Nothing," Delan said quickly, waving one hand dismissively. "Don't mind me, I get maudlin. What did you mean before? How I can bear it? Bear what?"

Lyander cocked his head, then remembered what he'd said. "Oh, yes. How can you stand living outside of walls, being out in the open?"

Delan coughed, surprised. "Are you serious?"

"Yes," Lyander answered. "Being in my garden is all I can bear of being under the sky, and I don't stay out there long even then. It's so vast. It's terrifying. You were a farmer?"

Delan laid down the crust of his bread and licked his lips before answering slowly. "Once, yes. Once, I was a farmer."

"So how did you do it every day? Under all that emptiness?" Lyander shuddered and looked down at his slowly-congealing stew. He pushed the bowl away, bringing his left hand forward before dropping both hands into his lap. "I've lost my appetite."

"It frightens you," Delan said, sounding incredulous. "It really frightens you."

Lyander nodded, rising and moving away from the table. His stomach churned at the thought of being trapped outside, unable to reach the shelter of the Temple, unable to hide from that enormous weight of *nothing*. He jerked in surprise as arms closed around him from behind, then relaxed at the sound of Delan's gentle voice in his ear.

"It's all right. I've got you, Lyander. You're safe. You're inside." He repeated it over and over, and Lyander felt his terror fading away like incense tendrils in the air. He turned in the circle of Delan's arms and rested his head on the other man's shoulder.

"I'm sorry," he murmured when he could finally speak again.

"Nothing to be sorry for," Delan answered, his hand moving in slow, comforting circles on Lyander's back. "I didn't know. Now that I do know? Well, I won't suggest taking any meals in the garden for a start!"

Lyander smiled and closed his eyes, resting his fingertips on Delan's waist and breathing in the musky, incense-and-spice scent of his skin. He moaned softly as Delan's hand dipped lower, skimming over Lyander's hip. Lyander pressed closer and was unsurprised to feel the heat of Delan's erection against his leg. Lyander raised his head to meet Delan's eyes and his smile widened.

"Where?" he whispered, feeling his own cock starting to rise. After their second couching, Delan had expressed a desire to pleasure Lyander on every possible surface in the Thraya. Lyander had been skeptical at first. After all, plain, quiet Delan wasn't someone Lyander would have expected to have talents in the arts of lovemaking. But what Delan didn't have in experience, he made up for with enthusiasm, and Lyander was starting to suspect the Temple sisters might have been coaching Delan when he was outside the Thraya. Delan's next statement confirmed the suspicions.

"One of the sisters found out I can read, so she gave me some books. To learn more for you," he murmured, leaning forward to kiss Lyander's lips, then his cheek. He laughed and added, "I never knew... didn't know anyone ever wrote about this kind of thing. Now I can't wait to try some of the things I've been reading about."

The unveiled eagerness in Delan's voice made Lyander laugh with him. He tipped his head back, offering Delan his throat.

"What kind of things?" he asked, closing his eyes in pleasure as Delan's teeth raked gently against his skin.

In answer, Delan chuckled and pushed both of Lyander's arms back, grabbing his wrists in one hand while doing something with his other. When he was done, he released Lyander's wrists and stepped back, grinning as Lyander discovered his hands were firmly pinioned at the small of his back.

He struggled for a moment, then looked at Delan.

"What did you do?" he asked, feeling his heart hammering against his ribs.

"Used a piece of wire to shorten your chains. I'll undo it when we're done." He stepped close enough to cup Lyander's cheek with one hand. "If you don't like it, tell me."

Lyander tugged against the chains, finding it somehow both disturbing and arousing to have no use of his hands at all. He met Delan's deep, brown eyes, saw the question in them and answered by turning his head to kiss the warm palm resting against his cheek. As he turned, Delan pulled him closer, taking his face between his hands and kissing him deeply. Lyander closed his eyes and moaned, feeling as if he was about to burst into flames as Delan slowly started pushing him backward until his back was against the wall. With Delan pressed against him, there was nowhere for Lyander to go. Nothing he could do but struggle and whimper as Delan's hands ran over his body, and his teeth and tongue explored Lyander's jawline, throat, and shoulder.

"Do you like this?" Delan whispered, pulling away slightly.

Lyander gasped as the pressure on his chest abated and staggered forward a step, hearing Delan laugh as he caught Lyander in strong arms.

"I take it that means yes?" he asked, running his fingers through Lyander's long hair.

Lyander nodded, his cheek brushing against the rough weave of Delan's shirt. He felt Delan kiss the top of his head, then his hands caressed his shoulders before moving down Lyander's back. He steered him until the backs of his legs hit the edge of the couch. He sat and watched as Delan stripped his shirt off over his head and dropped it to the ground, the lamplight silvering the scars that marked his chest and back. His trousers followed, revealing more of the marks about which Delan refused to answer any questions. Delan reached down and drew Lyander back to his feet, running his fingertips over the jeweled belt of the loincloth.

"Shall I take this off?" he asked.

"Yes, please," Lyander whispered, pressing against Delan's body. "I like being bare for you."

"You realize you're already mostly naked every time I see you," Delan answered with a laugh, finding the catches and letting the silk panels fall to the floor. He ran his hands up and down Lyander's sides, over his hips, finally letting them rest at Lyander's waist. "It's maddening."

"Then I'll be all naked for you whenever you see me," Lyander offered. "I like when you look at me."

"Just look?" Delan teased, stepping back and crossing his arms. "Is that all you want me to do?"

"Delan!"

"As if I could." Delan stepped forward again, pushing Lyander down onto the couch and kissing him. He crouched over Lyander as his hands explored the familiar territories of Lyander's skin. Lyander arched and squirmed under Delan, wanting more, gasping, and unable to find the words. The only word he could manage was his lover's name.

"Delan," he moaned. "*Delan!*" Then he found another word. "Please!"

"What do you want, my lovely one, my Lyander?" Delan whispered, his hands resting on Lyander's shoulders and pushing him down. "What should I do to you?"

Pinned, completely unable to move, Lyander looked up at Delan and whimpered, "Anything. Everything. Please!"

Delan smiled. He leaned down and kissed Lyander gently, then stretched out next to him on the couch. "There's the problem. I can't think what to do with you first." He ran one firm hand down Lyander's chest. "I don't have much time, so I suppose I'll just have to fall back on my old favorites." Delan kissed Lyander's bare shoulder. "I forgot the oil."

He got off the couch and limped over to a set of shelves, picking up a bottle as large as both his fists together. He carried it back to Lyander, looked down with a grin, and uncorked the bottle with a flourish, pouring scented oil over Lyander's naked chest and belly.

"What are you doing?" Lyander asked.

"Anointing you. Worshiping you," Delan answered, his voice thick with lust. He knelt over Lyander's legs and started smoothing the oil over Lyander's skin. "Loving you."

Lyander closed his eyes as Delan continued the massage – long sweeping strokes over his belly and chest, his shoulders and throat, then back down until Delan's hand closed around Lyander's cock. It was so very good as Delan toyed with him, one hand busy on Lyander's shaft, the other playing with his nipples. All the while Lyander strained and struggled, gasping and moaning, knowing Delan was not going to let him spend. Not yet.

"Delan, please!" he stammered. "Please, now!"

"Are you ready, my Lyander?" Delan asked. "Are you ready for me?"

"Yes. Yes, please."

"Good. Because I'm more than ready for you," Delan said.

He stopped what he was doing and shifted, moving off of Lyander's legs and helping him to roll onto his side. Delan kissed his hip, then moved away again, coming back with several cushions. When he was done, Lyander was laying over the pillows, his ass raised, his knees spread wide. He gasped at the cold trickle of more oil as it ran down his back, only to have it be warmed almost immediately by Delan's hands.

Another massage up and down Lyander's back and arms left him relaxed and whimpering in pleasure, a soft counterpoint to the jingling of chains as Delan's hands brushed against them. Above him, Lyander heard Delan laugh, then his oil-slicked hands moved down over his ass, a massage that grew increasingly more intimate, until the hands fell away and were replaced by the warmth of Delan's body.

"I can't wait any more," Delan groaned, and Lyander heard a wet, slicking sound that he realized was Delan preparing his own cock. Lyander tried to turn, tried to see Delan, but was blinded by his hair. "I'm ready to burst for want. Tell me you're ready."

"B-e-eeen... been ready." Lyander gasped. "Please, Delan!"

Delan groaned and pressed hard against Lyander's ass, his fingers digging into Lyander's right hip. Lyander forced himself to try and relax as he felt something hot and slick probing against him, pressing too hard, too fast. He whimpered, and Delan stopped.

"Easy, love. Easy," Delan whispered. He slowed, pulling back slightly, then moving in again more slowly. "Sorry. Too eager. Are you all right?"

"Yes. Yes, Delan."

"Should I continue?"

"Yes, Delan!"

Delan laughed and pushed forward again, slowly filling Lyander until his hips rested against Lyander's ass. He started pumping, thrusting again and again until Lyander was panting and moaning, his eyes closed tightly. He tugged hard on his wrists, wanting to move and touch, but helpless to do anything. Being bound was nothing new, but being completely at someone else's pleasure, unable to even touch himself, was deliciously intoxicating. Lyander howled as he crested, hearing Delan's deep, familiar rumbling gasps as he came a moment later. His movements slowed, then Delan went still, his hands warm on Lyander's skin for a moment before he shifted, leaning over and kissing Lyander's back. Then he withdrew and helped Lyander lay down flat on the couch before stretching out next to him and pulling Lyander into his arms.

Chapter 2
Outside the Doors

"You're magnificent," Delan murmured, kissing Lyander's mouth, then his forehead.

"You are, too." Lyander sighed, happy and sated, curling against Delan's warmth with his head resting on Delan's shoulder. "I'm curious. You never shout," he added, rubbing his cheek against Delan's shoulder, feeling the scar there like ropes beneath the skin.

"Hmm?"

"Jyase, the others. They would shout when they came. Make some kind of noise. You don't. Why?"

Delan yawned, his fingers tracing idle designs on Lyander's back. His voice was sleepy when he answered, "Taught myself not to."

"Whyever for?"

"Because if you get caught, you get punished," Delan answered absently.

"What?" Lyander tried to sit up and couldn't, as Delan's arm tightened around him.

"What? Wait, what?" Delan blinked and looked around, slipping his arm out from underneath Lyander. He sat up and rubbed his hand over his face. "Damn, was I talking in my sleep?"

"You said... something about being punished if you got caught?" Lyander said. "Caught doing what? Having sex?"

"It's nothing, Lyander. It was long ago, and it doesn't matter anymore." Delan lay back down, this time facing Lyander, pulling him close and running one firm hand down Lyander's side. "No one is being punished here."

Lyander nodded, hearing that note in Delan's voice that he'd come to understand meant there would be no answers if he asked any more questions. Instead, he tugged on his chains and smiled. "Are you going to let me go?"

"Let you go? Never. Release your hands?" Lyander felt Delan shift, felt him doing something, and he could move his hands. He stretched his arms as much as he was able, then turned and curled up against Delan, tucking his right hand back up behind his back so he could rest his left on Delan's stomach.

"I wonder what it would be like for you to hold me," Delan said, his voice husky, stroking Lyander's tangled hair with one hand. "I wish I could take the chains off of you."

Lyander shook his head, yawning slightly before he answered, "You can't. The chains can't come off. Ever."

"But I've seen you at the sunset meditations with your arms free," Delan protested.

Lyander nodded, resting his cheek on Delan's chest, running his fingers over another of Delan's scars. "When I'm needed in ritual and I need my arms, they chain my ankles," he said. "It's part of the mysteries, Delan. I really can't explain it to you. Just accept that I won't be able to be unchained. As much as I'd like to hold you, it wouldn't be..." He sighed.

"Wouldn't be what?" Delan asked. "Lyander?"

"I'm sorry. I can't say more. I've said too much as it is."

Delan grumbled but didn't press. Lyander felt fingers running through his hair again. He was just starting to doze when Delan jerked, almost tumbling Lyander off of his chest.

"What?" Lyander asked.

"Fell asleep. We should get you bathed before meditations." Delan rose, helping Lyander to his feet. He then led the way to the inner door of the Thraya, the one that led deeper into the temple, to the sunken bathing chamber fed by underground hot springs. In the pool, Lyander relaxed in the chest deep waters and let Delan bathe him, combing the tangles out of his hair. Twisting the long length into a tail and draping it over Lyander's shoulder, Delan kissed the back of Lyander's neck. His wet hands slid over Lyander's sides, and Lyander stepped back into Delan's arms, resting against his chest.

"Is there time?" he asked, looking up and back. "For you to have me again?"

"Not tonight," Delan answered, leaning down to kiss Lyander gently. He kept his arm around Lyander as they walked out of the water. "But I promise I won't be late tomorrow."

Lyander laughed, watching as Delan picked up a drying sheet. "Can you come back after meditations?" he asked as Delan rubbed him dry. "Can you stay with me tonight?"

"Stay the whole night?" Delan asked. "You've never asked that before."

"I've never asked that of anyone before. But I liked sleeping with you there, having your arms around me. I want you to stay. Will you?"

"If you want me to come back, I can ask permission." He kissed Lyander gently and smiled. "I liked it, too." He wrapped the sheet around Lyander's shoulders, then stepped back to dry himself off before going to the door. As it opened, a chilly draft chased around Lyander's bare ankles. He saw the evening lanterns, bespelled to start glowing at sunset, flickering in the hall, and saw Delan frown.

"Wait here," Delan said. He walked away, and was back a moment later. "Lyander, it's full dark out there."

"It is?" Lyander gasped. "But..."

"I know. Someone should have come to fetch you for sunset meditations. Where are they?" Delan looked around, then shook his head. "Let's get you dressed. Maybe... maybe they're just late."

"How can you be late for sunset?" Lyander asked, coming over to join Delan at the door. He tried to look out into the room, but Delan stood in the way, keeping Lyander from coming out of the bathing chamber.

"I've no idea, but—" Delan broke off and turned, his eyes wide as he stared off toward the doors that led out of the Thraya.

Lyander heard something and was about to ask what was wrong when Delan grabbed his arm.

"Be still!" Delan snapped, dragging Lyander back into the bathing chamber and closing the door. "Do you trust me?"

Lyander didn't have time to react, let alone answer the question as Delan stripped the drying sheet from his shoulders. He tossed it into a corner, then forced him back into the waters. They splashed into the deepest part of the pool, into a corner where the shadows were darkest. When Lyander started to ask a question, he was stunned to find himself pinned with his back against Delan's chest and with one of Delan's hands clamped over his mouth.

"Be still!" Delan hissed into his ear.

Lyander nodded as best he could, then gasped as he heard crashing from outside the bathing chamber.

Delan muttered softly, then whispered, "When I tell you to, take as deep a breath as you can and hold it. Do not fight me. Trust me. Understand?"

Lyander nodded again.

"Now!"

Lyander gulped in as much air as he could. A heartbeat later, Delan dragged him underwater, down to the very bottom of the pool. Lyander squeezed his eyes shut and tried to ignore the burning he could feel in his chest, the ever-increasing need to breath. It had become almost too much to bear when he felt the hand over his mouth fall away, felt Delan's hand on his chin, turning his head. Then Delan's mouth closed over his. They breathed together for far-too-short a time, then Delan pulled back, clamped his hand over Lyander's mouth as he slowly let them both rise to the surface. As they broke through, Lyander wheezed and sputtered, the sounds muffled by Delan's hand.

"Stay here. Stay down and be ready to duck back under," Delan hissed in his ear. Lyander nodded, and Delan let him go, slipping silently through the water toward the door. He crouched there for a moment, one ear pressed to the wood, then opened it and peered out. Finally, he let out a long breath and relaxed. "It's safe," he said, turning toward Lyander. "They're gone."

"Who?" Lyander demanded coming out of the water. "Delan, what happened?"

Delan looked back at him, his eyes dark and cold. "Men. Men in armor. I saw them when they came into the bathing chamber. I don't think they saw us, though. Lyander, I think the Temple has been taken. We need to find a way out of here."

Lyander shook his head, feeling as if everything was wobbling around him. "That isn't possible. The Temple cannot fall—"

"I didn't say fall. I said it was taken." Delan rose and picked up the drying sheet. He wrapped it around Lyander, rubbing his hands up and down Lyander's arms. "They were hunting for you, Lyander. I need to hide you until Eldest Sister gets control of what is going on outside." He grimaced and looked around. "You don't have anything I would call real clothing. And those damned chains... we'll have to do the best we can. Come on."

"We can't hide in here?" Lyander asked. He tucked his left hand behind his back and held the drying sheet closed with his right, following Delan out of the bathing chamber. Just past the door he stopped, staring at the wreckage he hadn't been able to see before, the debris that had once been couches, tables and chairs. "Delan!"

"That trick will only work once. And look at this. They turned over and destroyed anything that a person might have been able to hide under or behind. They really want you," Delan said grimly. He went to the door that led to Lyander's enclosed garden and disappeared outside. He came back a moment later, shaking his head. "I might be able to climb that tree, but I don't see any way you could alone. Maybe if I belt us together..." He paused, frowning, then shook his head. "No. My leg wouldn't take the strain. There has to be another way."

"Why are you so sure they want me?" Lyander asked, picking his way slowly through the debris. "They could be thieves—"

"There's enough gold and precious gems in the sanctuary and the common areas to satisfy any thief," Delan interrupted. "There's no need for them to come this deep into the Temple if all they wanted was gold. Why they came this deep, I've no idea. No one outside the temple even knows you're here." He hunted around, then tugged his trousers out from underneath a toppled bookshelf. Pulling them on, he frowned. "I don't see your loincloth anywhere. Buried, most likely. Come with me. I want to see if we can get you up that tree."

"You're joking!" Lyander protested. Delan turned, and his serious expression was enough to silence any other protests Lyander could have made.

"Lyander," he said softly, meeting Lyander's eyes and holding them. "I'm trying to protect you. But I can't do that if you won't help me. Trust me, and let me take care of you. Please?"

Stunned by how serious Delan had become and by the idea that someone had broken into the Thraya, Lyander nodded. "I trust you. What are we doing?"

"I'm going to see if I can get you up that tree," Delan repeated. "It might take me getting behind you and pushing. I don't know. If I had some way to break that chain I'd do it, and mysteries be damned." He held up one hand to stop Lyander before he could say anything. "I know. I know! Come on." He turned and headed toward the garden door, and Lyander trailed along behind him, hesitating a moment at the threshold. He took a deep breath, closed his eyes, and stepped out into the cold, night air. When he opened his eyes, Delan was looking at him.

"This is going to be hard for you. I know that. I wouldn't ask this of you if we had a choice," he said softly. "Let the sheet go. It'll only be in the way."

Shivering, Lyander did as he was told, moving closer to Delan for both warmth and comfort. "Now what?"

"Do what I tell you," Delan answered. He took Lyander's arm and led him to stand beneath the only tree in the garden, an ancient willow tree with branches that arched up over the towering wall. There, Delan stopped, scowling at the tree. "This isn't going to be easy," he said softly.

"What do I need to do?" Lyander asked.

Delan smiled at him and pointed.

"Put one foot there. I'll help you."

Lyander swallowed hard and did what Delan told him, fumbling clumsily as he attempted to climb without use of his hands. Delan tried keeping his palm on Lyander's back, catching him when he tottered and would have fallen, and cursing enough for the both of them when it became patently obvious his plan was not going to work.

"I'm sorry," he said as he brought Lyander back into the Thraya. Lyander just shook his head, trying not to show how badly his teeth were chattering. Delan looked at him, then walked away, coming back with one of the fur robes that had once been strewn over Lyander's couch. He wrapped it around Lyander's shoulders. "And I'm twice an idiot for taking you out there in that cold with you wearing nothing," he added. "Lyander, I'm sorry."

"I'm fine," Lyander said. "I'm just cold."

"I'll make up a bed for you. We'll get you bundled up, and I'll see if I can think of something else." Delan dug around, coming up with armloads of furs and silk that he fashioned into a nest on the floor. He helped Lyander lay down, then piled more furs on top of him.

"Delan, how did they get in? Did they break the locks on the door?" Lyander asked, huddling under the furs and slowly starting to feel warmer.

Delan shrugged, picking his way carefully across the Thraya. He stopped and righted the table, shaking his head as it tipped back over before he answered, "Maybe. Or they got one of the Sisters to open it."

"Do you think they would have left it open?" Lyander yawned as warmth started to turn to lethargy. "If they thought the Thraya was empty?"

Delan looked at him, then at the door. "It's worth a try," he said. "I should have thought of that first." He started toward the door, and was halfway there when it abruptly swung open and admitted a tall armored man who was carrying a naked sword. Delan backed up a step, and Lyander struggled to sit up, pinned down by the weight of the furs. He *knew* this man, knew every expression on that beautiful face, the way his smile lit up his eyes. The way his dark hair drooped down over his forehead when he leaned down over the table. He knew every expression but this one – he'd never seen that hardness before, or the cruelty.

"Jyase!" he said.

Jyase turned at the sound of his name and smiled when he saw Lyander.

"I told them they were idiots. That you had to be here," he said. He glanced at Delan. "You're the new caretaker?"

"Yes," Delan said slowly. "So you're Jyase?"

"He told you about me?" Jyase sounded surprised. "I'm flattered."

"What are you doing here?" Delan asked, slowly moving toward Lyander. His eyes, Lyander noticed, never left Jyase. "The Sisters told me you left to join the army."

"I did," Jyase agreed. He smiled, the crooked grin that Lyander had always found endearing. "I am." He turned to shout over his shoulder, "I found him!"

Delan cursed, and it took a moment for Lyander to figure out why. When he did, he moaned softly. "You? You're with the people who attacked the Temple? Jyase, why?"

Jyase looked at Lyander and laughed in a way that made his skin crawl. "Little Lyander. Lovely little Lyander. Are you bare under there, sweet? I've missed you—"

"Leave him be!" Delan growled, stepped in between Jyase and Lyander. "What do you want?"

Jyase looked evenly at Delan. "My Lady-General wants the treasure of this temple."

"Fine. Take the fucking gold and go."

Jyase laughed. "Really? You have no idea, do you?" As he spoke, six men filed into the Thraya. They fanned out from the door and stopped, waiting. Jyase didn't turn. He pointed his sword at Lyander. "There's the treasure of the Temple, caretaker. Right under your nose." He smiled again, and spoke to his men, "Take him."

Chapter 3
The Heart of the Temple

D elan rolled onto his stomach, tried to rise, and collapsed as pain shot through his aching head. He could smell blood, and knew it was his own. He and Lyander never had a chance.

He'd tried, though. Goddess knew he had. Tried and failed. The same way he'd failed before. But no... Delan's last memory was of Lyander screaming his name. Lyander was still alive. Delan pushed himself up onto his hands and knees, and stayed there for a moment, his head dangling between his arms, trying to find the strength to stand. Help. He needed help. Lyander needed help as well. There was still a chance to save him.

It was that thought that finally drove him to his feet, to stagger out the wide open Thraya door and into the hallway. There was no one there; no Sisters, no invaders. No bodies. Where was everyone? Was he the only one left alive?

The hallways seemed to go on for miles as Delan shuffled and stumbled toward the sanctuary. The familiar pain in his bad leg almost drowned out by the pain in his head. Everything seemed to fade in and out of focus, and he could feel warmth trickling down the side of his face. Lyander. Sweet, innocent Lyander.

Who needed him. He would find help. He wouldn't fail. Not again.

At the door to the sanctuary, Delan stopped, leaning hard against the lintel and panting, wanting to cry. No one here. No one alive, anyway. There were bodies here, women he'd known and admired, who had helped him and taken him in when he'd had no place else to go. The Holy Mother herself lay before the altar...

"Someone let us out!"

Delan heard the shouting and turned, almost throwing himself off balance as he tried to locate the source of the sound. Where? And who?

"Can anyone hear me?"

Brina, Eldest Sister, and the Temple war-leader. They'd left her alive? He almost smiled. Now they had a chance! He staggered toward the sound and found himself standing outside a heavy door. Inside, someone was pounding hard on the wood.

"Is someone out there?"

Delan didn't answer. With shaking hands, he fumbled at the lock, then shot back the bolt and tugged the heavy door until it started to move. Immediately, whoever was inside pushed and the door swung wide. Brina strode out, only to stop dead in her tracks and stare.

"Delan?" she gasped. "Warrior, where's Lyander?"

"Taken." Delan croaked, "Took... Jyase... he took..." That was all he managed to get out before the pain overwhelmed him. His bad leg collapsed under him, and he never felt himself hit the floor.

When he woke again the pain was gone, and he could feel tightness around his head that spoke of bandages, and the slight disjointed feeling he associated with deep magical healing. The last time he'd felt this way was after his leg had damn near been cut off. He looked around, saw he was in his own tiny room, and sat up.

"He's awake, Holiness," someone outside the curtain that served as his door said.

"Thank you." To Delan's shock, Brina walked into the room. No. Brina never walked. She stalked, like a hunting cat. Delan had been shocked by her when he'd first met her – he hadn't known women could look like her. He'd met warleaders before, but they'd all been tall, impressive looking soldiers. Brina reminded him of a brick wall – she was about his height, and as soft as the stones the Temple was built from. He could see that she and Lyander were related, but comparing the two of them was like comparing a willow tree and a thorny stump.

Once he'd gotten over the shock, he'd liked her immediately.

"Did you find him?" he blurted out, not bothering with honorifics or propriety. "Did you find Lyander?"

Brina shook her head slowly. "You didn't give us much to go on. What happened?"

"You don't know?" Delan groaned and rested his head in his hands. "It was Jyase, the caretaker before me. He came back for Lyander. He said his Lady-General wanted the treasure of the Temple." He watched Brina as her face lost all color. "Brina, what did he mean?"

"Something he shouldn't have known. Something Lyander himself doesn't know. That means..." She paused and her eyes narrowed. "I'm going to filet that bitch," she snarled.

"What bitch?" Delan demanded. "Brina, what's going on?"

"Nothing. It is nothing you need worry about, Delan. It is—"

"Let me guess," Delan interrupted. "One of the mysteries?"

Brina looked startled. "Yes. How did you know?"

Delan shook his head and slowly got to his feet. "Brina," he said softly. "They're going to kill him, aren't they?"

She met his eyes and nodded briefly. "Probably. His worth as... as a sacrifice is immeasurable."

He closed his eyes and swallowed, standing up straighter. When he opened his eyes again, Brina was watching him curiously.

"I'm coming with you when you go after him," he said flatly.

Her eyes widened.

"This doesn't involve you," she answered. "You're not one of us."

"Maybe not, but I'm coming with you all the same. He... Brina, I'm not going to fail him. I promised him I'd stay with him, that I'd take care of him. I'm going after him. With or without you."

"Delan—"

"No, you don't understand," Delan said quietly. He started to pace, the pain in his faltering stride a welcome distraction from his own guilt. "He asked me tonight if I was a farmer before I came to the Temple. I told him only half the truth. I *was* a farmer until I was fifteen. Until I was picked up out of my father's fields by one of the warbands. My General was a good sort, not like the scum that attacked the temple. She was out there trying to protect the people from the ones like the lot that did this." Delan gestured widely, taking in the entire temple in one wave of his arm. "For five years I was a soldier, until I took a lance in my leg that damn near took it off entirely. I came home to find my family dead, and my grandmother's farm burned to the ground.

That was... well, that was when I came here. I had no place else to go." He turned and looked at Brina. "I spent the last five years protecting people like Lyander. But I couldn't protect the ones that meant the most to me. I couldn't protect my family. I wasn't there. I was right in the Thraya with him and I still couldn't protect Lyander. He's out there right now, somewhere, and he's terrified. Did you know that? That he's afraid of being outside? I... I can't just leave him! And I'll be damned if I'm going to abandon him." He stopped, then folded his arms over his chest. "Is that involved enough for you, Brina?"

Brina nodded once. "You could've just told me you were in love with him. Come along, I'll see you outfitted."

DELAN FOLLOWED BRINA through the Temple halls, into a part of the Temple where he'd never been allowed access. "I'm sorry," he said after a long silence. "About the Holy Mother."

Brina looked over her shoulder at him. "Thank you," she said quietly. "I'm trying not to think about it. I don't have the luxury of grief. Not yet."

"I understand," Delan said. "Where are we going? The armory isn't down here."

"No, it isn't. But if you're going to be fighting for us, for Lyander, then you should know what you're fighting for," Brina answered. "In here." She led him into a room dominated by a large stone fountain in the center.

Delan walked up to the fountain, watching the water spill and play in the basin.

"Brina—?" he started to ask, and his question was cut off when she grabbed him by the back of the neck and dunked his head into the water. He came up gasping and cursing. "Lady's Tits, woman! What was that for?"

She snorted and answered, "Language, Your Holiness."

The title penetrated his sputtering invective and he stopped, staring at her. "*What* did you call me?"

"Congratulations. You're the first Priest of the Mysteries in five generations," Brina answered. "Now I can tell you what you need to know."

Delan shook his head slowly, water splattering the ground as it streamed from his wet hair. "No. No, no, I can't be a priest. I... I can't."

Brina frowned in confusion. "Why ever not?"

"There aren't any Warrior Priests," Delan sputtered. "And if there were, they wouldn't take *me*. Not... not someone like me. I... Brina, I never told you the truth. Never told anyone here the truth. I was afraid I'd be put out. But... I'm anathema."

"Anathema?" Brina asked softly. "Delan, I think you'd best explain. Since no one witnessed this but me, we can deny that it happened. You can walk away, but that means walking away from Lyander. So explain."

Delan ran his hand through his wet hair and silently cursed himself once more. "I don't know how I can be any more clear. I'm anathema—"

"Says who?"

"The village priestess, my father, my grandmother—" Delan answered. He looked down and shook his head again. "I... they wanted me to marry. I didn't want the girl. I didn't want *any* girl. I never have and never *will*. They tried to pray it out of me and when that failed, they tried to beat it out of me. That's most of my scars. The ones that didn't come in battle. I let them think it worked, and, well, my General saved me from the marriage. But d'ye know what it's like outside the Temple? If you're born like I am? They stone you to death if they find you with another male. If you're lucky. If they want to make an example out of you, they use pikes..." Delan swallowed and wiped his hands on his pants, feeling his gorge rising. Zekial. Poor, besotted Zekial. Delan had warned him, tried to get him to be careful. He'd tried to get him to see that the miller's boy hadn't been safe. But Zekial hadn't listened, the poor fool.

"Do they?" Brina asked slowly. "I'm going to have to do something about *that*. I wonder if Mother knew?" She shook her head. "We can't worry about that now, though. Delan, there isn't anyone in this temple who would call you anathema. We don't believe that what you are is a sin."

"You don't?" Delan said, his voice shaking with disbelief. "But my father—"

"Probably wasn't born in the shadow of the Warrior," Brina finished. "That whole 'males are damned unless they're under the control of women' is an idea that came with the Holy Wars and the damned Priestesses of Light. Delan, the daughters of the Warrior consider being jinsal—"

"What?"

"Jinsal. It means you prefer your own sex," Brina explained. "Lady bless, Delan, half the women in this temple are jinsal! Within the Temple it's considered to be holy. It also tells me that you were God sent. You're the person we need to save Lyander. Come with me and I'll show you why." She turned, going to the far wall of the room.

On the wall there was an empty torch bracket, and she reached up and turned it firmly. Delan felt rumbling under his feet and heard the groaning of old machines as a section of the wall slid back and away, revealing a hidden corridor.

"What do you know of the Holy Wars?" Brina asked, taking a lit torch from another bracket.

"Only a little." Delan followed her into the dark hallway. "My village had a temple school, but I wasn't allowed to go. It was females only. The only reason I know how to read is because my sisters taught me."

"Ah. Your entire village was of the Light? Well, very quickly then. Did you know this was once two temples?" Brina asked over her shoulder. As she walked, Delan noticed the space was opening up. They'd gone from a corridor into a large room. "The second temple was actually the reason for the wars. Because the Priestesses of Light—damn them all to the coldest level of perdition—objected to the existence of a God. Men were inferior, they said, and had to be controlled."

"Now you sound like my father and grandmother," Delan said. "Where are we?"

"The Temple of Lyas, the Sorcerer." Brina stepped forward, lowering the torch to a shelf that stood at about waist-height. At once, a tiny flame raced away from them, following a channel Delan supposed must have been filled with oil. It split, then split again, until the room glowed with light, and Delan could see clearly the statue that dominated the room.

The figure was carved from what looked like a single piece of marble, twice as tall as a man. He was nude, and proudly male, and Delan was intimately familiar with every curve, every line, every part of that body.

"That... that's Lyander!" he said in wonder.

Brina shook her head. "No, that is Lyas, consort to the Warrior and keeper of the Mysteries."

At the word, Delan turned and looked at her. "You said that I was a Priest of the *Mysteries*. Not of the Warrior."

"You are now a Priest of the Mysteries. Sworn to Lyas. A Lyan Priest, if you like. Since you're the only one, I suppose that makes you High Priest by default," Brina said.

"This is too much. I don't understand." Delan turned to face Brina. "And we don't have time for me to understand. Just promise me you'll explain?"

"So you're staying?" Brina asked.

Delan nodded slowly. "For Lyander, I'm staying."

"In that case, I'll talk fast. Come on, let's get you armored."

"THE THRAYA IS QUITE possibly the oldest part of this building. It's a legacy of the old Temple, the one that existed before the wars," Brina said as they left the statue behind and headed back the way they'd come. "The Priests of Lyas were cloistered. It hadn't been used in decades until Lyander was born."

"He said he didn't remember there ever being another man in the Thraya," Delan said.

"There never had been. Not in his lifetime," Brina said, and glanced over her shoulder. "Delan, there hasn't been a male born to a Warrior Priestess in our entire history. There is something in the vows that we swear, something in the consecration that ensures we bear only daughters. That held true until Lyander."

She opened the door to the armory and led Delan inside. "We must have some male armor in here somewhere."

"Chain mail would work."

"That we have." Brina opened a chest and started pulling things out. "When Lyander was born, we had no idea what was happening. We're not even sure who his father was. Our seers couldn't tell anything about why we suddenly had a male in our midst. But there had to be a reason, so we kept him. Raised him. Then Lyander started to get older. He lived in the main temple with the Temple sisters until his voice broke and he started to dream. That was when his magic woke."

"Men don't have magic," Delan said absently, examining a sword hanging on one of the racks. "This one ... this is different. I've never seen a sword like this before."

"Take it. If it calls to you, it is meant to be yours. And you're only part right," Brina said, shifting rattling armor around in a chest. "Here. This should fit you. Gambeson are over here."

Delan turned and took the chain mail shirt that Brina offered. "I'm not going to be much good in a fight, Brina. This leg of mine..."

"We'll have the healer work on it again before we leave. Men don't have magic anymore, Delan, because Lyas was the source of men's magic. According to the lore, when the Lyan Priests were all taken and killed by the Light bitches, that was at the same time that the God Lyas was destroyed by the Goddess Fersina of the Light. It was then that men's magic vanished from the world. Until now." Without a hint of self-consciousness or shame, Brina stripped above the waist and started pulling on padding and armor. Delan felt his face grow warmer, and turned his back as he rummaged through the gambeson until he found one that fit him.

"Lyander was thirteen," Brina continued. "He started to dream about sex, started to become a man, and his magic ripped through the halls like a storm. That is why Lyander goes chained. To contain his magic, lest it consume him."

"Why does his magic need to be contained?" Delan asked. He picked up the chain mail and shimmied into it, wincing as his hair caught in the rings and pulled. He settled the armor with a sharp twist of his hips, then picked up the sword and belted it on. He looked around, helped himself to a bow and a quiver of arrows, then asked, "Is there a helm that will fit me?"

"The racks are behind you," Brina answered. "And the Holy Mother believed his magic is so powerful because he bears all of it. All of the magic that once was born by men is held by Lyander. She believed he is truly Lyas, reborn in a mortal shell and, ah... what happens when you fill a bucket, Delan?"

"If you fill it too full it overflows," Delan answered immediately.

"And if it is a sealed cask?"

Delan blinked and realized what she was saying. "It bursts."

"Good. Think of Lyander as that sealed cask. He's filled to overflowing with magic, with all of the power of a reborn god. Mother thought she might be able to siphon some of that power off, but we didn't have another to share the load. Not until now. Now we have you."

"What?" Delan jerked around and stared at her, nearly dropping the helm he had chosen. "I don't have any magic!"

"You will. You had all the signs. Your mother was a mage, wasn't she?"

Delan shook his head. "I don't know. She died birthing me." He cocked his head to one side. "But my grandmother used to call her a witch. I thought it was just that she didn't like my mother. But maybe..."

"Perhaps there was more to her than you know. You have potential. The Holy Mother saw it when you came here, or she'd never have let you stay. Come on. If you've got everything you need, grab a belt knife. All right. Let's see the healer. Then we'll see what we can find for horses. Hopefully, they left us something."

Chapter 4
The Man who Fights

The healer, an older woman who had never had more than two words for Delan before, exclaimed over him and treated him as if he were her only son, coddling him until he was ready to scream with impatience. But when she was done, his leg felt better than it had since before that last disastrous battle.

"Whoever saw to this had the skill of a butcher," she said with a dismissive sniff. "If it were me, I'd have put it to right and you'd still have two good legs." She patted Delan on the knee. "All right. You're as fixed as I can make you right now. When you get back, we'll see about doing more."

"You should forgive Mags," Brina said as they hurried toward the stables. "She's not usually that forward."

"Mags? Oh, you mean the healer?" Delan nodded. "I noticed. That's the most she's said to me since I got here."

"Yes. Her own daughter was stillborn a day or two before Lyander was born, so she acted as Lyander's wet-nurse. Then she never bore another living child. She's very fond of Lyander."

"How does she know where we're going?" Delan asked.

"She has eyes, Delan," Brina said, sounding amused. "We're armed to the teeth after an attack on the Temple where they took a single prisoner. Where else would we be going?"

They pushed the stable doors open and were welcomed by a chorus of whinnying horses. Brina sighed with relief.

"I was worried they'd have either stolen or killed the horses," she said as they gathered up tack. "That we'd be going after them on foot. You can ride, can't you?"

"I can," Delan said grimly.

"What were you in the warband? And which warband?"

Delan was silent for a moment, focusing on saddling the horse he had chosen. Then he answered, "Arthemia was my General. And when I rode with her at the end, I was her second."

"You?" Brina gasped. "Holy Mother... Delan... I always thought it was an unusual name. That's because that's not your full name, is it? Your name is Markedelan!"

Delan looked up sharply at sound of the name he hadn't heard in months. "How did you know my name?"

"*You're* the Man Who Fights?"

"All men fight. Some of us are more open about it. How did you know my name?"

"Arthemia was one of us!" Brina answered. "She rode on the order of the Holy Mother, one of the only warbands we could muster to try and do right by our people. She was the War-leader here in the Temple before me. Oh, Warrior, if I'd known... she *told* us about you. About the male who could have been a warleader of his own merit. About how she wanted to bring you back, to have you dedicated to Lyas! Why didn't you tell us your full name? And why didn't she send you to us when you were hurt?"

"Because she died," Delan said softly. "That was how I took the injury—trying to save her."

"Warrior hold her." Brina breathed. "We didn't know she'd fallen. It would be months between her letters at times." She slapped her horse firmly on the neck, then shook her head. "Time to mourn is later. Now, we need to ride."

"What are they going to do to him, Brina?" Delan asked as he mounted his horse.

"If we're lucky, all they'll do is sacrifice him," Brina answered, leading the way out of the stables. "That will release the power he contains and probably kill them all in the process."

Delan felt as if a rock had settled in the pit of his stomach. He didn't want to know, but he had to ask regardless." And if we're not lucky?"

Brina looked back, her face was bleak in the torchlight. "They'll break him first."

THE CART BUMPED HARD and the swaying stopped. Lyander moaned in pain behind his gag and instinctively tried to shift, tried to hide. Ropes dug painfully into his arms and legs, and he stopped struggling. There was no way to move, no way to escape. Nowhere to go, even if he could get free of the ropes layered over the temple chains his captors hadn't bothered to remove. Jyase and his men had taken him from the Temple, cutting down anyone in their path, and presented him to a woman whose face was hidden by her helm, who had nodded without a word and ridden off.

They hadn't followed her. Not immediately. It seemed that Jyase had other plans. He let his men sport with their chained captive, and they passed Lyander back and forth among themselves, toying with him as if he were a doll, laughing over his struggles and helplessness. When his protests and pleading grew too loud, they gagged him, and continued with their tormenting, until at last Jyase strode through the crowd, whipping them off as if they were dogs fighting over a bone. He'd taken Lyander and dragged him off toward the cart, and for a moment Lyander had thought that his ordeal was over.

Jyase had shown him otherwise. And it was worse. So much worse when it came at the hands of someone that Lyander had trusted. Had loved. He'd fought, remembering things Delan had explained to him, and had managed to land one lucky kick, knocking the wind out of Jyase.

That had been the reason for the beating. Jyase had used a strap, then his fists, and Lyander wasn't certain he could have moved even if he hadn't been bound. He certainly couldn't have run. Jyase had focused most of his attentions with the strap on the soles of Lyander's feet.

Outside the cart, Lyander heard voices coming closer. One of them was Jyase—Lyander would know his voice anywhere—the other was a woman. As they came closer, he heard her voice clearly. "It hasn't yet been violated?"

"No, Mistress. I stopped the men before they got that far."

"Good. I want this to be a complete victory over the pretender god. We destroyed the false priests, now we will destroy the vessel. Bring it to the altar and prepare it for sacrifice. I've looked forward to this day for a very long time."

IT WAS A CLEAR NIGHT, and the newly-risen moon was bright enough to turn the frost-covered ground to a glittering pathway. Which made the trail the raiders took clear. The dark path was a gash cut through the diamond-studded sedge. Delan tried not to consider it an evil omen and urged his horse forward.

"How long was I unconscious?" he asked.

"Not too long. The attacks happened at sunset, just as we were preparing for sunset meditations. When did they breach the Thraya?"

"Just after full dark," Delan answered. "I noticed it was dark when we came out of the bathing chamber. We hid underwater the first time they came through." He frowned down at his reins. "I wasn't ready for the second time."

"You can't blame yourself, Delan," Brina said firmly.

"How did Jyase know?" Delan demanded. "How did he know what Lyander is if it's part of the mysteries?"

Brina growled slightly. "Did the Holy Mother tell you when you came to the temple that you were not to dally with the Sisters?"

"Yes, I remember telling her it wouldn't be an issue. She thought that was funny," Delan answered. "Why?"

"Because one of the Sisters was sleeping with Jyase, and apparently telling him things he should never have known," Brina said. "That was why he was turned out. The little idiot was bearing his child."

"Oh," Delan said. He frowned and thought about it. "Why was that a problem?"

"Because as Lyander's attendant, he was supposed to cleave only to Lyander. He betrayed the oath he swore and we turned him out." Brina looked at him curiously. "You didn't swear an oath?"

Delan licked his lips. "Honestly, I can't remember. I probably did, but all I remember was being told there was a young man in the Temple, and I was not only encouraged to lay with him, it was *expected* of me! I thought I was dreaming."

Brina snorted, amused, and Delan turned his attention back to the road. "There! They turned off there!"

"Can you tell how long ago?" Brina asked.

Delan dismounted and awkwardly went to one knee studying the ground, the frost-bitten grasses and the broken stems.

"Things are starting to freeze again," he said after a moment. "Not too long. We're catching them." He looked up at Brina. "What happens when we do? There were at least six of them. I'm not good for more than two or three, I think."

"We'll know when we get there," Brina said softly. "Mount up."

"Do you have any idea where they're going?" Delan asked, hauling himself back into his horse and following the trail. "I don't know this ground."

"I think so. There was a cloister up here once. A school, if you will. For young men who had just entered Lyas' service. So they could learn sorcery without being a danger to anyone." Brina's voice carried through the still, night air. "I've read about it, in the archives. When the Light bitches attacked at the beginnings of the last battle, they struck the school first. It was a massacre. By the time the Sisters knew and could get a defense force up here, it was too late, and two hundred men and boys were slaughtered like cattle."

Delan's brow slightly furrowed as he tried not to think of Lyander suffering the same fate. "So this land once belonged to the Temple. Do you know the area?"

Brina turned in her saddle and glanced at him. "Pretty well. We'd drill out here. Why?"

"They're probably using the ruins of the cloister as a base, I would think," Delan answered. "Is there anywhere we could check the lay of the land without being seen?"

Brina nodded and turned back, urging her horse forward. "I know a place. It will be hard to get there, though. We won't be able to take the horses in. Are you up for rock climbing?"

Delan fought back a grimace. "I can do it."

Brina said nothing in response. She simply led the way to a hidden cave where they left the horses. Then she tied a rope around her own waist and offered the other end to Delan. He took the rope, tying it off firmly, bracing himself as Brina tugged on her end.

"From this point until I tell you otherwise, not a word," she murmured. "These rocks echo."

Delan followed Brina as she scrambled up the side of the cliff. She went slowly, pointing out footholds and handholds as she went, pausing often so Delan could gather himself and catch his breath. But still, by the time she led him into a level pocket of the cliffside, Delan could taste the blood in his mouth from where he'd bitten his lip to keep from crying in pain.

"Should've left you at the bottom," Brina whispered into his ear as she untied the rope.

"And if you didn't come back? Where would we be?" Delan answered, his voice pitched low. "I'm fine. I'm used to this. Now, where are we going?"

Brina snorted and gestured, crawling further into the shadows, then out onto a flat ledge. She lay down and waved Delan up next to her. He stretched out flat, burying his face in his arm to hide the tell-tale tendrils of his breath in the cold night air, and looked out into the valley. There was a clear view of the ruined cloister below, and of the camp that had been erected in what once must have been a courtyard. There were torches ringing the tent, that clearly lit the area; Delan frowned counting tents, campfires, sentries, then nodded and tapped Brina's arm. They crawled backward into the pocket, and Delan slumped against the rock wall.

"I counted maybe twelve," he said softly. "Two by the fire, three by the wagon, two on patrol on the near side of the ruin, two on the far side, possibly three inside that large tent. What happened to the rest of them? It would have taken more than a dozen to take the Temple."

"They don't need a warband for the ritual. They were probably sent back to their base. How did you see inside?" Brina asked.

"Shadows. There's a fire inside and when they passed in front of it, I could see their shadows where the wall had fallen. One of them was a woman, I think."

"I'd be surprised if there wasn't at least one Priestess down there," Brina murmured. "Count on at least one acolyte, too. Those damned Light bitches never travel alone. Twelve is too many. How do we do this?"

Delan blinked, startled out of his pain-filled stupor by the question. "You're asking me?"

"You're the Man Who Fights," was the surprising answer. "Arthemia told us that you had a way with tactics the like of which she'd never seen before. So... what do we do?"

Delan scowled, leaned back against the rocks and closed his eyes. "I don't know the terrain, I don't know their real strength or their weapons. I don't even know if Lyander is in there! How am I supposed to plan an attack when I don't have all the information?"

"Do your best," Brina answered. "That's all you can do."

"That's what she always said." Delan sighed at the memory. "Arthemia. She told me the same thing."

"She learned it from our mother," she replied. "I'll leave you to think."

"Wait," Delan said. Brina turned toward him, silent as a stone. "You know what they're going to do, don't you?"

"I have an idea..." she hesitated. "I've heard about their Dark ritual. They'll break him before they sacrifice him. Torture, possibly rape. Then the sacrifice will be with the dawn. Is that what you needed to know?"

"Yes," Delan answered. Brina moved away into the shadows, leaving him alone. He grumbled, then crawled back out onto the ledge and stared down into the ruin. He lay there long enough that the cold seeped through his clothes, sinking into his bones and making them ache. But by the time he finally shook himself and crawled back to find Brina, he knew there were actually fourteen people down in the ruins, that only two of them were women, that the eight sentries were lazy and incompetent.

And from the screams that suddenly shattered the frozen midnight stillness, Delan knew that the torture had started.

Chapter 5
On the Offensive

B rina took the first two of the sentries, moving like smoke through the trees and killing the men with almost casual ease. Delan followed behind her, his bow held ready, feeling the calm quiet he remembered so clearly from his days as a soldier. The calm before the battle, Arthemia had called it, the first time he'd described it to her. The signs of a true warrior, one worthy of her time and attention. Privately, Delan doubted her assessment—he was male, after all—but he'd paid careful attention to Arthemia during the times when she instructed him, and he remembered. Now, hopefully, all those long hours would pay.

Brina rose from the body of the second sentry and glanced at Delan. He waved her on and followed, trying to move as silently as she and failing miserably, until they reached the edge of the wood. This close to the ruin, they could hear laughter from within—a woman's laughter, and loud, ragged sobbing. Delan growled softly at the sound, fury overwhelming his calm.

"Easy, Delan." Brina breathed into his ear. "We can't help him if we're dead."

Delan nodded, closing his eyes and taking a long breath, letting the cold air damp the fires within until he could think clearly. He nodded once more, touching Brina's arm. She patted his shoulder and slipped away into the darkness, moving around one side of the clearing. Delan went the other way, listening intently.

He found the next sentry easily enough. The man had built a tiny fire in a tiny hollow underneath a tree, and was crouched over it, holding his hands over the little blaze for warmth. He obviously heard Delan approaching. His head jerked up at the sound of branches and leaves crackling. But he didn't move from his fire, instead pulling a pipe out of his pouch and lighting it with an ember. Delan smelled the acrid sweetness of dreamweed, and managed to bite down on a sigh of disgust. *Morons.* The sentries were all morons. How did they expect to hold the ruin if they didn't have competent people to defend it?

Delan frowned at the thought, then shook his head. He put an arrow to the string, drew, and fired. The sentry fell with a bolt in his throat, and his body smothered the little fire.

Delan moved on.

Halfway around the clearing, the sounds from the ruins went still. Delan froze, then heard the warbling of a night bird. A moment later, Brina appeared out of the shadows.

"It got quiet," Delan whispered.

"They'll keep him alive until dawn," Brina answered, her voice sounding strained. "They're either leaving him alone or he's passed out."

"Pray to the Warrior you're right. How many sentries?" Delan asked her.

"Four."

"There were three on this side," Delan said. "That makes nine with the two you killed on our way in."

"One of mine was taking a piss. Maybe he was from inside?" Brina suggested.

Delan nodded, scowling as he silently counted corpses. "There are only five left," he said. "One of them is the Priestess. One of them is Jyase. Is he a good fighter? He didn't attack when they took me down. He let his men do it."

"I don't know. He didn't take weapons training with me," Brina said. "Do you think you can take him?"

Delan thought back to the Thraya and seeing Jyase. How he moved, how he held his weapon and how he carried himself. An evil suspicion bloomed. "Brina? How did he come to you?"

"Same as you did. Showed up around the first snow, looking for a place. Why?"

Delan swallowed past the lump in his throat. "Who taught him? He knows how to fight. He knows enough at least to know how to move. He's been trained. I didn't get any weapons training until I met Arthemia. I've never heard of a male getting real weapons training, even if the warlady meant for them to be expendable. But just here we had eleven of them, even if most of them were idiots. And there were others at the Temple. So who trained them? Who trained Jyase?"

Brina went very still, then started swearing softly under her breath. "You're saying he was *planted*? That he knew what he was looking for?"

"I think so, yes," Delan answered. "Was he the first caretaker?"

"No. Before him there was Anaki, and before Anaki was Trivir," Brina answered. She frowned. "Anaki was with us for most of a year and left us to marry when his village sweetheart came looking for him. He lives with his wife and children about five miles east of here. They come to the Temple now and then to visit, and they named their oldest boy Lyan. Trivir... he was the first boy we brought in. He was a nice boy, but a little simple. He went home to take care of his mother after a half a year when she became ill. Their village was razed a few months later. Lyander doesn't know."

"Was he killed?" Delan asked.

"We never found him or his mother," Brina said. "You think he told?"

"Given what Jyase knew, I think it's likely. And if you all thought Trivir was simple, I'll bet you weren't as circumspect as you should have been. We had a scout like that, she could make people think she was cloud struck, and they talked around her as if she weren't there. We learned more from her in a week than we did in months of surveillance." Delan shook his head. "Right, so we can be pretty certain that Jyase was sent by the Light to confirm whatever they'd learned from Trivir. He knew about Lyander. And he probably seduced the girl so that he'd have a reason to get thrown out of the Temple. I just don't understand why!"

"Why what?"

"Why go through all the trouble. Why spend years, at the very least, in training men to be warriors, then send them into the Temple to find someone who may not really have existed."

"To destroy Lyas completely." Brina answered. "If he can be reborn once, he can be reborn again. But what happens if he dies while he's mortal? If Lyander dies without ever assuming his full potential?"

"You... you tell me. What happens?"

Brina shook her head. "I don't know. But I imagine they think that if Lyander dies, Lyas dies. Forever."

Delan swallowed. "They've been planning a long time for this."

"Probably since the Lyan priests fell. They must have guessed Lyas would rise again. So they've been waiting for a Temple son, just in case. They'd have taken Lyander even if he wasn't Lyas reborn. Come on. They'll notice that other one is gone before too long."

They stopped under cover at the edge of the clearing, close enough to the tent that they could hear movement from within. Delan pulled his scarf up over his mouth to hide his breath, and nudged Brina until she did the same. From inside the tent, they could hear a woman, her voice high-pitched and angry-sounding.

"Wake him up!" she shrilled.

The answering voice was low, male, and Delan thought it might have been Jyase. "I've been trying!"

"He needs to suffer more. He needs to break before dawn!"

"I know!" It was definitely Jyase, and he sounded annoyed.

Delan winced as the clear sound of a slap rang through the clearing.

"Do not dare take that tone with me ever!" the woman snapped. "Who do you think you are? Do you think just because we put a sword in your hand, that you're important? That you're equal to even the least of the Sisters?"

"I brought you the pretender god!" Jyase protested. "Does that mean nothing?"

"It means you're an exceptionally useful male, but you are still just a male," the woman said, her voice thick with contempt. "You are chattel, like a stallion or a bull, good only for the strength of your back and the potency of your seed. And perhaps not even for that. I think perhaps this has given you an elevated sense of your own worth. Perhaps when this is all over with and the Light reigns supreme, it will be time to temper you."

Delan shuddered, hearing Jyase moan and start to beg. "No, Serenity! Please, I... I'll remember my place. Please... it was the moment, and frustration that... that I could not fulfill your wishes. Please, forgive me. I will make amends."

"You will. On your knees, dog, and show me how contrite you are. You will not rise from that position save at my command."

"Yes, Serenity."

The sounds that followed were clear, the sound of a woman taking her pleasure. As the Priestess' moaned and cried her climax to the night, Delan turned away and saw Brina arch an eyebrow at him. He leaned toward her, pressing his head against hers.

"What did she mean?" Brina whispered. "Temper?"

"She means to geld him," Delan answered.

Brina nodded, then gestured away from the tent. Delan followed her back into the undergrowth, until they were far enough away from the clearing that he felt safe taking his scarf from his face.

"That's a high-ranking Priestess, or I'll eat my armor," Brina said as she sat down facing him. "Possibly the High Priestess herself, the bitch. I can't see her entrusting this to any of her subordinates. One of them might get airs and try to overthrow her."

Delan looked back the way they'd come. "No one's noticed the missing sentry. Isn't that odd?"

"The males have all been idiots. I'm not surprised—" Brina started to say, but stopped, cocked her head to the side, her expression thoughtful. "The men have all been idiots," she repeated.

"I thought so, too," Delan agreed. "One of the ones I took down was smoking dreamweed and had built a fire."

"It's as if they didn't know what was expected of them," Brina continued slowly.

"Perhaps they didn't?" Delan suggested. "Conscripts from surrounding farms, forced into arms."

"I'd say maybe, but there are strong penalties for smoking dreamweed in the villages around here. This trash came from further afield."

The answer hit all at once. "Delinquents," Delan said. "There are delinquency camps for incorrigible males, or so my grandmother claimed. She used to threaten to send me to one at least once every moon. From what I've heard, they do whatever they have to do so that they can break a male and remake him into something properly submissive."

"I've heard of them," Brina said softly. "And dream heads would be sent there, wouldn't they? So they're using delinquents? Addicts, bandits, thieves, those sorts of men."

"It makes sense," Delan agreed. "Why some of them seem to know what they're doing, and why none of them seem to care what happens to the others. Why no one has come looking for the missing. I wonder how many have run off already?"

"Enough that she doesn't seem to think it worth looking for the one who left the camp and never came back. Or perhaps that's just because he's simply a male. Warrior, I'll never understand how they can think so little of you."

Delan didn't answer. It didn't seem to warrant an answer when he had never understood it either. "It will make it easier to run the rest of them off, though. If they feel no loyalty to the Light, then they won't stay around when we attack."

"Do you have a plan?" Brina asked.

Delan leaned back against a tree thinking furiously. The man he'd killed came to mind, crouched over his tiny fire, smoking the deadly weed.

"Yes. I have an idea."

THE DROUGHT AND THE drying frost made the entire wood a potential tinderbox, and the challenge was not in starting the fire, but in not burning too much and having the flames rage out of control.

"We want this to burn itself out, not take the whole area," Delan said as he and Brina worked to stack the deadfall just so.

"You've done this before," Brina accused.

"Once. To flush out a group of raiders. Just..." He frowned, looking at the bonfire-to-be. "We had a mage with us. She made it look like a lightning strike, to hide our position. It was useful, being able to start the fire from someplace else."

Brina heard the question he wasn't asking, and answered it, "I don't have that kind of power. That's why I'm a warrior. My magic is very basic."

"Do I have that kind of power?" Delan asked. "You said Holy Mother saw the signs on me, and I'm a Lyan priest now. If I'm the High Priest to the god of male magic, that means I should have some kind of magic myself. Doesn't it? So is that something I can use?"

Brina looked stunned. "I... don't know!" she stammered. "This... this is virgin ground for me, Delan. I've never worked with a male mage before."

"Well, forget I have a cock and imagine me with tits then," Delan suggested. "How do I start?"

The last thing he expected was Brina to start giggling, then whooping with laughter, muffling the sound with her hands and her scarf until she managed to get herself under control. Once she had, she wiped her eyes and shook her head.

"I'm sorry," she murmured. "But you'd make a damned homely woman, Delan."

"Can we get on with this?" Delan snapped.

Brina snorted, taking a long breath and stepped forward.

"Right. May I touch you?" she asked.

Delan nodded, and Brina lay cold hands on either side of his face, closing her eyes. It was something that the Holy Mother had done the day Delan had come to the Temple, something he hadn't questioned at the time. Now, though...

"What are you doing?" he asked.

"Hush. Let me see. Oh. Oh, yes. You do have potential. Can you feel me? Feel what I'm doing?"

"No... wait. Yes, I think so." Delan closed his eyes and frowned, feeling something. *Heat? Pressure?* He wasn't sure, but there was definitely *something* inside his head. Just to see, he pushed back, and heard Brina snort once more.

"Good. Very good," she murmured. "Most of the time beginners can't even do that much. All right. Watch what I do."

Delan wasn't certain what she meant, until the presence in his mind moved. He followed it, amazed, until he found himself standing at the edge of something.

"What is this?" he asked

"Where you end and everything else begins," Brina answered. "This is where you set your ground. Think of it as your foundation. Once this is set and ready, we'll go further."

Delan nodded, following Brina's directions. He growled in frustration as she easily knocked aside his first attempts. "Do we have time for this?" he demanded.

"It's been less time than you think," Brina answered, sounding amused. "Listen."

Delan did as he was bid, and heard a long, deep thump, as if someone had sounded a sustained note on a drum. There was a long pause, then he heard it again. "What is that?" he asked.

"Your heartbeat. Working like this only seems to take a long time. Now rebuild that ground!"

Finally, Delan had built something Brina could not knock over, and she pronounced passable. "Now, you're ready to tap into the lifestream."

"The lifestream?" Delan repeated. "Ah... is that where the magic comes from?"

"Yes. And I'm not sure if this is going to work. Or how to show you how to do this. The lifestream is a very female thing." Brina hesitated, then asked, "Tell me what you see?"

Delan looked around, confused. "I don't see anything."

"There's no river? I see a river, just over the edges of my awareness. That's the lifestream."

Delan moved back to the edge, looking down into what Brina had said was the beginning of everything. "I don't see anything. Why a river?"

"Because women's magic and women's cycles are tidal," Brina answered. "Oh... I see. Or rather, I don't. There's nothing here for you to tap in to."

Delan opened his eyes and found himself back in the winter woods. "Because Lyas hasn't returned. No men's magic. So we're stuck. I have magic, but I can't use it. Not until we know what I'm supposed to be doing."

"And we won't know that until we save Lyander," Brina finished, shaking her head slightly as she reached into her belt-pouch and brought out her tinderbox. "Well, then. We start the fire the usual way."

"Give it to me," Delan said, holding his hand out.

"I can start a fire, Delan."

"I've no doubt, considering you remembered to bring a tinderbox and I didn't. How are you at setting a fire so that it burns slowly?"

Brina looked at him, then handed him the tinderbox. Delan went awkwardly to one knee and set the tiny fire, hiding it behind part of the deadfall. He examined his work for a moment, picked up a larger piece of wood and sniffed it, then set it into place. He got slowly to his feet. "We should have enough time to get back to that cover we had before."

"Good. What then?"

"We'll see."

Chapter 6
Freed

By the time they'd reached the cover closest to the ruins and the tent, they could hear the torture had started once more. Delan flinched at the unmistakable sound of a whip cut through the air, followed by muffled cries of pain.

"They've gagged him," Brina murmured. "Oh, Mother, what has he ever done to deserve this? The poor innocent."

"We'll get him out," Delan whispered. "We'll bring him home. We'll help him—"

The rest of his thought was cut off by a distant popping sound. Delan turned and saw a red-gold glow and billowing smoke.

"Must have been pitch pockets in the wood," he said softly as he drew one of the remaining arrows from his quiver and set it to the string of his bow. "Hopefully, not too much. I don't want the whole forest to go up in flames, but with it this dry, it just might."

"What was that?" the Priestess inside the tent demanded. "Maris, go and see."

A young woman appeared, and Delan was close enough to see the front of her white robes were liberally decorated with blood. He glanced at Brina, who nodded.

The arrow took the priestess in the back of the neck, and she fell without a cry, but the sound of her body hitting the ground was enough to draw the attention of one of the guards. This time, Delan's aim wasn't as good, and the guard screamed as he fell.

"Shit!" Delan swore as he pulled another arrow free. He drew and released in a single smooth motion, and a second guard fell. He heard crashing from behind them, heard Brina engage. More noise coming toward him fast, and he turned and used the bow to barely block a blow from a club that would have crushed his skull. It did shatter the bow, and Delan threw the broken pieces at his attacker as he rolled away and drew his sword, expecting to have his brains bashed in at any moment. But the attack didn't come. The man stopped with his club raised, then looked over Delan's head and went pale.

"Fire!" he shouted. He glanced at Delan, cursed, turned, and ran.

"That was easy," Brina muttered, breathing heavily.

Delan got to his feet and looked at her, there was blood on her sword and more on her sleeve. She dismissed it with a shake of her head. "Not mine. That was the last guard, wasn't it?"

"Unless I counted wrong," Delan answered. "Now it's just Jyase and the Priestess. Which do you want?"

"Oh, give me the Light bitch." Brina almost growled.

"She's yours. Let's get done and get out of here before that fire catches us." Delan said as he moved out of the bushes and toward the tent, stopping when Jyase appeared. The other man looked at him, clearly surprised.

"Well, if it isn't the little caretaker," Jyase said. "Thought we killed you."

"I don't die easily," Delan replied.

"We'll see." Jyase laughed and drew his own sword.

Delan tuned out the sounds of the fire, popping and crackling in the distance, and the much closer sound of the Priestess shouting in alarm for her guard. Now, there was only Jyase.

Jyase smirked, then lowered his head, starting to circle to his right. "No attacks?"

"You first," Delan answered, his movement mirroring Jyase's, his sword coming up to guard. *Watch the eyes. Watch the eyes, not the blade. Watch the shoulders.* He saw Jyase's arms tense and was ready, blocking the blow easily, even though the strength behind it made him stagger back a step. He was still ready for the next blow, though. And the next, and with that third blow, Delan recognized the pattern, and realized Jyase knew nothing at all about real sword fighting.

"They taught you by the numbers, didn't they?" Delan called, feeling the smile starting as Jyase went pale. "You poor bastard. They gave you just enough slack in the leash that you thought you were free."

"Are we fighting or talking?"

"Do you want to be free?" Delan asked. "Put your sword up. Help me bring him home. You cared for him once—"

"I lied," Jyase snapped. "I lied to him and to all of them. And the idiots believed me."

"Then run," Delan said. "Because I'll kill you if you stay."

"Really? A cripple like you?" Jyase attacked again, a thrust Delan knew was the next attack in the number sequence. He parried easily and attacked in earnest, the unconventional fighting style that Arthemia had pushed him to learn. Delan saw the panic in Jyase's eyes as the man struggled to defend himself.

Panic that only grew as Delan got through his guard time and time again, until his sleeves and trousers were sliced to ribbons and streaked with blood, and his breathing was ragged and filled with pain.

Delan stopped, meeting Jyase's eyes. "Yield, and I'll let you live."

"She'll kill me. If I let you live, she'll worse than kill me." Jyase gasped. "Better to die."

Delan sighed. "All right." He attacked again. This time to his shock, Jyase didn't even try to defend himself. Delan's sword struck at the juncture of his shoulder and neck, slicing clean through his throat. Jyase fell backward, made a horrific gurgling noise, then fell still.

Delan stood for a moment over Jyase's body, panting hard. "You poor bastard," he muttered, then looked around. "Brina!"

No answer. He couldn't hear anything, which left him with no idea where Brina was, or the Priestess. He didn't care, either. Right now, he needed to get Lyander. He turned and stumbled into the tent, gagging at the thick smell of blood and incense.

The first thing he saw was the altar; a rough structure of wood and stone that looked as if it had been cobbled together from debris found in the ruin. There were tools on the surface; a whip, a knife, other things that Delan couldn't even put names to. The blade of the knife was still wet with blood. Lyander's chains were there, too, the shackles broken. Beyond the altar was a brazier, and beyond the brazier...

"Lyander!" Delan rushed around the altar and past the brazier. They'd hung Lyander by the wrists from the ridgepole, and he dangled there, his feet barely brushing the ground, seemingly unconscious, so badly beaten Delan couldn't even begin to catalog his injuries. He gingerly touched Lyander's arm, and was startled when Lyander moaned.

"Lyander. Lyander, it's me. It's Delan," he whispered softly. "I'm going to get you down. This... this is going to hurt." He wrapped one arm around Lyander's waist and tried not to hear Lyander's muffled scream at the touch. He stretched and used his sword to slice through the ropes, then let his sword drop to the ground as he gently lowered Lyander to lay across his legs. And finally, for the first time, saw Lyander's face. His breath caught and he closed his eyes for a moment before fumbling for the scarf around his throat. Slowly, he wound the cloth around Lyander's head, covering the bloody ruins that had once been his eyes.

"It's all right, Lyander," Delan whispered as he cut away the cloth they'd used for a gag. "It's all right. I've got you now. You're safe. I'm going to take you home. It's going to hurt, and I'm sorry, but we're going home, and Mags will make everything right." As he spoke, he examined Lyander quickly, taking stock of his injuries. He'd been whipped, more than once. His hands were blackened and charred, and the fingers looked as if they'd been broken before they'd been burnt. And his legs... Delan's own leg ached in sympathy. Even if Mags was the healer she claimed to be, there was no way that Lyander would ever walk again without pain. Delan licked his lips and turned away, back to Lyander. "Mags will make everything right," he repeated. "And we'll fix the Thraya up again, make it like nothing ever happened. And... and I'll stay there with you. I'll get Brina to make it so I can stay with you. Live with you. You and I, we're never going to be apart again." Gently, he touched Lyander's cheek. "I love you, Lyander."

"Delan?" The word was a bare whisper.

"Yes, Lyander. It's me. I've got you."

Lyander shifted, gasping as he raised his still bound wrists. "Free... free me?"

Delan nodded, then cursed silently. Lyander couldn't see him. Would never see him again. "Of course," he answered, his knife already sawing at the ropes. He heard the tent flap open. "Brina, he's hurt. We're going to need to rig a litter—"

"Drop the knife."

Delan jerked and looked up to see the Priestess standing on the other side of the altar.

"Drop the knife," she repeated. "Then be a good boy and put that on the altar."

"Fuck you," Delan spat. He jerked the knife, and the ropes parted. Lyander's hands fell limply to his chest. Delan ignored the Priestess' indignant squawking, touching Lyander's cheek once more.

"Lyander? You're free."

To his surprise, his words drew a weak laugh from Lyander. "Free," he repeated. "Delan?"

"Yes, love?"

"Love you. So very much."

Before Delan could say anything, Lyander groaned. His body spasmed, then went rigid, his back arching off of Delan's legs. Then, like a string-cut puppet, he went limp in Delan's arms.

"Lyander?" Delan gasped. "Lyander!" He dropped his knife and fumbled at Lyander's throat, hearing the Priestess laugh.

"Oh, is the poor little Abomination dead?" she asked as she came around the altar, her voice heavy with mocking sympathy. "A pity. I was hoping it would live until sunrise. Well, then I suppose the only thing left to deal with is you."

Delan froze, realizing he was unarmed, and with Lyander's body across his legs, pinned down. There was nothing he could do to stop her.

And he really didn't care. He looked back down at Lyander and rested his hand on the still chest, the quieted heart.

"Go ahead," he said, not looking up. He took a long breath, let it out slowly, and closed his eyes. "Kill me. I won't stop you."

He heard her cruel laughter. "Well, then. Since I have permission. Not that *your* permission matters ..." Her voice trailed off. "What... what are you doing?"

Delan blinked and saw immediately what she meant. Lyander was... glowing? His arms tightened around the body, and the glow grew brighter. "I'm not... what the *fuck*?" The glow grew even brighter, enough that Delan had to squint. He refused to look away, refused to let go. "He's already dead, woman!" he shouted. "Leave him alone!"

The Priestess sounded as confused and frightened as Delan. "This isn't anything I'm doing!"

Brighter and brighter still, until Delan held a small sun in his arms. A small sun that without warning shattered into a million shards of light and left Delan's arms empty. Delan yelped as several of them passed through his body, leaving behind only warmth. The Priestess was not so lucky. A single shard pierced her breast, and she fell to the ground like a stone.

The light faded, and Delan sat there for a moment, breathing hard, wondering what had just happened. Then he heard something hit the roof of the tent. A single, solid, *plop*. Then another. Then more, coming faster.

"It's... it's raining?" he stammered, struggling to his feet. He picked up his sword and his knife, sheathing both before walking out of the tent and looking up in wonder.

It was raining golden drops of light.

Glittering, glowing droplets showered down from a cloudless sky, building to a downpour the likes of which Delan couldn't remember having ever seen in his lifetime. He walked out into the middle of the clearing next to the tent and stood there, his head tipped back, letting the rain wash over him.

"Delan!"

At the sound of his name, Delan turned, drawing his sword as he spun, only to pull up as Brina staggered toward him. There was blood on her face, running down her neck as the rain sluiced over her skin. "Delan!" she called again. "You're alive!"

"Appears so," Delan answered, sheathing his sword again.

"And... Lyander?" Brina asked as she came closer. Delan shook his head once, and she stopped, resting her hand on his arm. "I'm sorry. I... I think he may have done it, though."

"May have done what?" Delan asked.

"What he was born to do," Brina said and looked up. "Released Lyas. Brought balance. Have you ever seen such rain?"

Delan shook his head, unable to speak for the lump in his throat, and suddenly glad of the rain. It hid the tears. He wondered if Brina was crying for the loss of her brother. It didn't seem so. Was he the only one who'd mourn?

"Tell me what happened?" Brina asked.

"He... he was dying when I found him. You don't want to know what they did to him," Delan answered, his words choked. "I cut him down. He asked me to free him, so I did. I... I told him I loved him. And he died."

Brina sighed. "He died free. And freeing him let him take on his true place. You did well, Delan. And at least he saw you."

Delan didn't look at her. He looked up at the light in the east. Dawn. "No. No, he didn't. The bitch took his eyes. Let's go home, Brina. There's nothing left for us here."

DELAN IGNORED BRINA'S attempts to draw him out on the ride back to the temple, until she fell silent next to him. All around them, the rain of light continued, drenching them both to the skin. For some reason, it wasn't cold, and there was an odd taste to the rain, to the very air, something Delan couldn't identify.

They reached the temple well after sunrise and were met by the surviving Sisters, who took the horses and escorted Brina and Delan inside. Delan allowed them to fuss, letting their voices wash over him as they helped him strip off wet armor and clothing, wrapped him in dry sheets and brought him warm clothes. The only voice that penetrated his fog was Brina's.

"Delan?"

He turned, frowned. "Yes?"

"You're not limping anymore," she said softly. "Had you noticed?"

Noticed? He'd noticed nothing since the rains started. Delan looked down at himself, at the leg he'd almost lost, and realized for the first time he was in no pain. That he hadn't been in pain since...

Since he'd been pierced by shards of light.

He turned away. "I'm for my bed."

"Delan?"

"Brina, just leave me alone."

She hesitated for a moment, then answered, "As you will."

In silence, Delan made his way to his tiny cell, to his lonely bed. But once he lay down, there was no sleep waiting. No peace. Every time he closed his eyes, he saw Lyander's battered, bloody body, his eyeless face. Finally, after an endless time of lying there, staring at the ceiling, Delan got up and left the room, walking through quiet corridors until he reached the doors to the Thraya. They were still unlocked, partially open. He walked inside, and found nothing changed from when he'd last seen the great, empty room. Smashed furniture and torn draperies still littered the floors. And there, off to one side, was the bed he'd made for Lyander, so many hours ago. He staggered over to it, curled up amidst the furs and silks and cried.

Chapter 7
To Serve the Sorcerer

B rina found him in the Thraya, waking him at sunset, her soft voice penetrating the dark, thankfully dreamless sleep he'd finally found.

"Delan?"

Delan opened his eyes and looked up, blinking. "Brina?"

"I thought I'd find you here. I told the Sisters to let you be, but I thought you might want to see this."

Delan sat up. "See what?"

"Come and see."

Confused and curious, Delan followed Brina out of the Thraya and down the halls toward the courtyard. Outside everything still dripped with water.

"How long did it rain?" Delan asked.

"Most of today. I sent a party up to the ruins, and it rained enough that the fires are out. And I checked our records before I came to find you. It hasn't rained like this since before I was born," Brina answered. "But that's not what I wanted you to see." She nodded. "They are."

Delan turned, and his jaw dropped when he saw the young men, sitting on the long marble benches that ringed the courtyard. There were a dozen of them at least.

"Who are they?" he asked.

"The first of your priests... Your Holiness. They started arriving about midday, and the last got here only about an hour ago," Brina answered. "Go talk to them."

Delan stared at her for a moment, then swallowed. "Brina, I..."

"For him, Delan."

Delan shuddered. Turning, he walked over to the first of the young men. Closer now, Delan could see that this young man couldn't have been more than sixteen. "What's your name, lad?" he asked.

The boy rose, looking nervous. "I'm Barnar, sir."

"And what brings you here?" Delan asked.

Barnar looked at the other young men and drew himself up. "The rain, sir. I... I was out in the rain last night. The light, it filled me. And I heard a voice calling me. Calling my name. Telling me to come. To serve the Sorcerer. It told me to speak to the High Priest. But I've never heard of a High Priest before." He stopped, gnawing his lip, then asked almost timidly, "Is that you?"

Delan paused just a moment, then nodded. "That's me. My name is Del... Markedelan. I'm Lyas' Priest. All of you saw the light and heard the voice?" He looked down the line, seeing the men nodding. "Well, then, come on inside. We'll find a place for all of you."

The young men entered the temple in a tight knot, almost as if they expected to be attacked. Brina fell in next to Delan as he followed them.

"Clean out the Thraya?" she murmured.

"No," Delan answered, his voice firm. "No, we're changing the world here. No more men locked away like slaves and prisoners. Lyas' Priests will serve next to the Warrior's Daughters, equally. They'll get the same education, the same training." Delan glanced to the side. "Is that a problem, Holy Mother?"

Brina smiled, taking his hand. "Not at all, High Priest."

EVERY MORNING, THERE were new young men in the courtyard, men who reported hearing the voice in the rain of light. Every morning, Delan welcomed them into the temple, forcing a smile, acting the father figure while feeling as if he were dying inside. Finally, at the end of his first year as High Priest, he could bear it no more.

"Let me go," he said to Brina. "I... this is killing me."

"I know. I've been watching you. You're like a wolf in a trap," she answered. She looked at him, her dark eyes thoughtful. "What of the boys? What will you tell them?"

"That I've gone looking for others. The ones who can't find their way," Delan answered. "They can follow me, once they're ready. Once they're more proficient in magic and weapons, and know the lore. Lyas' Priests should walk the world. They have to, if they're going to change it." He felt his face grow warm and looked down. "I've given this a lot of thought."

"I can see that," Brina said wryly. "All right. We'll tell them at sunset."

The next morning Delan set out on foot, carrying only a pack and his sword, hearing the Temple voices, mingled male and female, bidding him farewell. He didn't care where he went, picking his roads at random. At every turn he found them, boys with their voices still breaking, men old enough to be his father, all of them saying they'd heard the voice on the night of the golden rain. He directed each of them toward the Temple, told them to tell the Holy Mother that Markedelan had sent them. Then he moved on. And as he walked, he found one burned out Light temple after another. In each town and village, the story was the same: on the night of the golden rain, the Light temples burned with a fire that gave no heat, and that could not be quenched by any means.

After the fifth such discovery, while sitting at his lonely campfire – one that he conjured by magic alone, something that never ceased to amaze him – Delan looked up at the darkening sky. "You have a truly evil sense of justice, don't you?" he called. "I like it."

As he fell asleep, he thought he heard laughter.

DELAN LOST TRACK OF the days, lost track of the number of young men he'd met and sent on their way. Lost track of the number of lost and bewildered former priestesses he met, and the number of times he was challenged by them. He lost track of the weeks, as he traveled roads he'd never walked before, and visited towns whose names were on no map he'd ever read. He camped in forests and fields, and shared meals with beggars and with great ladies. He spoke to all of them, telling them of Lyas the Sorcerer, of Fersina's betrayal, and the God's rebirth. He showed them his hard-won skills at men's magic, healing the sick and injured. Some of them scoffed, some of them laughed, some of them turned on him in scorn. All of them listened. And some of their sons took the road to the Temple. He lost track of time completely, until finally, Delan decided he, too, must take the road back to the Temple.

It was just after dawn, on the morning of midsummer. Delan was already up and moving along roads he remembered too well. The day was hot already, and promised to be hotter still by midday. Best to travel early, find shelter from the heat, then go on when the evening coolness gathered, before the late sunset. With luck, he'd reach the Temple after dawn tomorrow. As he came over the crest of the hill, he saw fields that had been barren the last time he'd come this way, and were now heavy with grain. And he saw a young man sitting in the shade of a bush near the side of the road.

"Markedelan," he called. His voice was familiar. Impossibly familiar, and Delan stopped in his tracks.

"Do I know you?" he called, his hand resting on the hilt of his sword. There had been one too many attacks that had started just like this. Then the young man rose and stepped into the light, and Delan felt his heart stutter to a stop.

"We've met," Lyander said. He was exactly as Delan wanted to remember him, smiling, beautiful, unchained and unhurt, wearing only the silken loincloth that Delan remembered so well. His dark eyes alight with mischief, and it took Delan several minutes just to remember how to breathe.

"You... you took your damned time." It was the first thing he could think of to say, and Lyander laughed.

"It's taken me a while to learn to do this," he admitted. "I've forgotten a great deal, living as a mortal. I came as soon as I could." He came closer, growing serious. "I'm sorry. I never meant to hurt you."

"It wasn't you that did," Delan said. "I never blamed you."

"I know. But still, I hurt you by leaving, and I am sorry. I... I can hold you now," he offered tentatively, and opened his arms.

Delan stared. He wasn't sure for how long, but long enough that the smile started to fade from Lyander's face. Long enough that Delan felt the sob welling up, the one that he'd been holding back for—how long had it been? Months? Years? He staggered forward and fell into Lyander's arms, pulling the other man close, burying his face in Lyander's hair.

"I missed you," he whispered. "I missed you so much." He pulled back, but only so far as it took to be able to catch Lyander's mouth and kiss him. The feel of Lyander's hands on his back, of that beloved body against his, was almost too much to bear. When he finally broke the kiss, he was panting, his cock achingly erect. "I'm going to shoot just from holding you," he murmured into Lyander's ear.

Lyander laughed, resting his head on Delan's shoulder.

"I've missed this. I've missed you," he whispered. "And holding you is as good as I'd hoped it would be. Oh, Delan, there are so many things I want to tell you."

"After."

"After?"

"After I take you off into the bushes and show you how much I've missed you," Delan growled.

Lyander's arms tightened, and he laughed again.

"You don't want a bed?" he teased. "There are thorns back there. And biting ants."

"Thorns and ants be damned. I don't want to wait until we can find a bed." Delan grinned and scooped Lyander up in his arms. "You fixed me, didn't you? The last thing you did for me was to fix my leg."

"And open you to your magic, yes," Lyander answered, twining his arms around Delan's neck. "And I have something to ask you, Delan."

"I told you. After." Delan started toward the side of the road. There was a thick stand of bushes not far away. It would be enough cover. Anyone within a mile would hear them, though. No matter...

"No. Now." Lyander ran his fingers over Delan's stubbled jaw. "I like this. Will you come back with me, my Delan?"

Delan stopped, suddenly confused. "Come back where? The Temple? That's where I was going."

"No. Not the Temple. Come back with me to the Heart." Lyander met Delan's eyes. "Where the gods live. You've served us truly and well, and the Mother of All has said I can have this boon if you agree—"

"Wait. Wait. Stop. Stop there. I need to put you down," Delan interrupted. He set Lyander on his feet and stepped back. "Explain. Mother of All?"

"Creator of the Gods. My real mother, if you will," Lyander answered. "No one worships her any more. At least, not around here. Her Temples were taken over by Fersina's followers a long time ago. Before she turned on me. Fersina wanted to be the only Power, and she was going to turn on the Warrior next. Until you helped break her power."

"Her Temples all burned," Delan murmured.

"That was me being petty," Lyander said wryly. "Not my best moment. But I like that you approved. That High Priestess? She was acting as a vessel for Fersina for that ritual. She had to. Nothing else would've killed me."

"So killing her killed Fersina?" Delan asked.

Lyander nodded. "For a time. She'll be reborn somewhere, at some point. And hopefully, she'll learn some manners when she does."

"Maybe she'll be born male," Delan said dryly.

Lyander giggled.

"Now that would be justice. I'll have to mention it to Mother."

"So you want me to come back with you?"

Lyander nodded. "Yes. Please. As... as my mate. My consort. My love. They already think you are, you know. That's what gave me the idea."

Delan frowned. "Who thinks what?"

"The people. Everyone you've talked to over the past ten years."

"Ten *years*?"

"You didn't realize? Yes, it's been ten mortal years," Lyander said. "I am sorry it took me so long."

Delan shook his head. "You said that already. Keep explaining. People think I'm what?"

"My Consort, walking the world on my behalf. They already think you're a God, Delan," Lyander answered. "They call you Markedelan, Beloved of Lyas. You didn't know?"

"No. No, I didn't," Delan answered. "And... if I do, what then?"

Lyander shrugged. "I don't know. It's never been done before. Wonderful things, I hope. You've already done wonderful things, Delan. Do you even know how many priests there are now?"

"I lost track a long time ago."

Lyander grinned. "I have, as of their last ritual, three hundred and seventy-three priests in various stages of training. The first twelve took Markedelan's road the spring after you did. And there are over seven hundred Sisters now, between new devotees and converts from the Light. You've done so much good. Mother says it's time you were rewarded."

Delan looked at him, at the smile he'd never stopped seeing in his mind, and laughed. He held his hand out, and pulled Lyander to him. "You're my reward. The rest... I don't care."

"You're going to become a magnificent god."

Delan grinned, nodded, leaned down, and kissed Lyander quickly. "After," he murmured.

"After?"

"After I make a magnificent god come."

ELIZABETH SCHECHTER has been writing award-winning Romantasy since before romantasy was a word. Her writing credits include the award-winning steampunk romance **House of Sable Locks**, the Celtic fantasy **Princes of Air** (recently rereleased as **Ravenborn**), and 2021 VIVIAN finalist **Written in Water.**

She was born in New York at some point in the past. She is officially old enough to know better, but refuses to grow up. She lives in Central Florida with her husband and son.Elizabeth can be found online at http://elizabethschechterwrites.com[1].

Subscribe to Elizabeth's newsletter at https://www.subscribepage.com/k4u7k2

---

1.   http://elizabethschechterwrites.com/

Don't miss out!

Visit the website below and you can sign up to receive emails whenever Elizabeth Schechter publishes a new book. There's no charge and no obligation.

https://books2read.com/r/B-A-KGBH-GYCJB

BOOKS 2 READ

Connecting independent readers to independent writers.

Also by Elizabeth Schechter

Heir to the Firstborn
Worlds Begin
Written in Water
Forged in Fire
Bones of Earth
Wings of Air
Visions in Smoke
Children of Dreams
Valley of Shadows

The Coral Throne
The Sea Prince
The Coral Throne

Standalone
The Rape of Persephone
Fools Rush In
Her Captive

To Market
Infernal Machine
Chains of Light
The Chronicles of John Zebedee
Snowbound

Watch for more at elizabethschechterwrites.com.

About the Author

Elizabeth Schechter has been writing award-winning Romantasy since before the word was coined. Her writing credits include the award-winning steampunk romance *House of Sable Locks*, the Celtic fantasy *Princes of Air,* and 2021 VIVIAN finalist *Written in Water.*

She was born in New York at some point in the past. She is officially old enough to know better, but refuses to grow up. She lives in Central Florida with her husband and son.

Elizabeth can be found online at http://elizabethschechterwrites.com, or on Facebook at https://www.facebook.com/Elizabeth.A.Schechter.

Subscribe to Elizabeth's newsletter at https://www.subscribepage.com/k4u7k2

Read more at elizabethschechterwrites.com.